Dirty Bertie

PIRATE!

For Lucy and Sam ~ D R

For Taylor ~ A M

STRIPES PUBLISHING
An imprint of Little Tiger Press
1 The Coda Centre, 189 Munster Road,
London SW6 6AW

A paperback original
First published in Great Britain in 2012

Characters created by David Roberts

ISBN: 978-1-84715-234-3

A CIP catalogue record for this book is available from the British Library.

Printed and bound in the UK

10 9 8

Dirty Bertie

PIRATE!

DAVID ROBERTS WRITTEN BY ALAN MACDONALD

stripes

Collect all the Dirty Bertie books!

Worms!
Fleas!
Pants!
Burp!
Yuck!
Crackers!
Bogeys!
Mud!
Germs!
Loo!
Fetch!
Fangs!

Kiss!
Ouch!
Snow!
Pong!
Scream!
Toothy!
Dinosaur!
Zombie!
Smash!
Rats!
Horror!
Jackpot!

My Joke Book
My Book of Stuff
Dirty Bertie Sticker and Activity Book
Dirty Bertie Pant-tastic Sticker and Activity Book

Contents

PIRATE!

CHAPTER 1

"AHARRRR!" roared Bertie, swishing his cutlass. It was Pirate Day at school and everyone in Miss Boot's class was dressing up. Bertie had always wanted to be a pirate. He would have his own ship – *The Black Bogey*. He'd live a pirate's life; plundering, looting and never washing behind his ears.

He marched in through the school gates. The pirates of Class 3 stood around, armed with plastic daggers and cutlasses. Eugene had a spotty scarf knotted round his head. Darren had a gold earring and a mouthful of black teeth. Captain Bertie greeted them.

"AHARRR, mates!"

"AHARRR!" they roared back.

Bertie jumped on to a bench and put his telescope to his eye.

"ENEMY AHOY!" he cried.

Over by the drinking fountain sat the weediest pirate alive – Know-All Nick.

Nick was Bertie's sworn enemy. Only yesterday he'd put chewing gum on Bertie's chair. Bertie had gone around all day with a big pink blob on his bottom. Well, now it was time for revenge.

"Fire one!" Bertie ordered. A tennis ball whizzed through the air and pinged off Nick's head.

DOINK!

"Nice shooting, lads!"cried Black-Eyed Bertie. "After him!"

"AHARRRR!" yelled Darren and Eugene, swarming forward like rats.

"OOO-ER!" yelped Nick, dropping his bag and legging it. But Bertie and his scurvy crew were too quick for him. In no time they had the enemy surrounded.

"HELP!" wailed Nick. "I'll tell Miss Boot!"

Bertie's cutlass poked him in the nose.

"Surrender or die!" he cried.

"I surrender!" gulped Nick, raising his hands.

Bertie rolled his eyes. It was no fun having a sworn enemy as cowardly as Nick. He always gave in without a fight.

"What shall we do with him?" asked Eugene.

"Tie him up!" said Darren. "Make him do sums!"

"Make him eat vegetables!" said Eugene.

But Bertie had a better idea.

"Start talking or we'll tickle your toes!" he cried.

Nick turned pale. He couldn't bear anyone tickling his feet.

"Please, not that!" he begged.

"All right," said Bertie. "Tell us where the treasure is."

"What treasure?"

"All pirates have treasure," cried Bertie. "Where did you hide it?"

WHAM!

Suddenly the school door flew open. The children gasped as a huge shadow fell over them. It was Miss Boot, the scourge of Class 3. She wore a feathered hat, enormous boots and a black patch over one eye.

"Yikes!" yelped Bertie.

"BERTIE! WHAT ARE YOU DOING?" thundered Miss Boot.

"Nothing!" said Bertie.

"HELP! Miss! They're being mean to me!" wailed Nick.

Miss Boot bore down on them like a galleon in full sail.

"IS THIS TRUE, BERTIE?" she boomed.

"It was only a game, miss," squeaked Bertie. "We're playing pirates."

"ENOUGH!" bawled Miss Boot. "Line up, all of you. Not you, Bertie, come here!"

She held out her hand. "I'll have that sword if you don't mind."

"But, miss, it's my cutlass," said Bertie.

"No weapons in class," snapped Miss Boot. "And that goes for the rest of you!"

Class 3 filed past, handing in their daggers and water pistols. Miss Boot took the weapons to her cupboard, where she locked them up.

"Get out your books," she ordered. "You will all do sums for the next half-hour. Anyone who talks will see me."

Bertie groaned. He bet real pirates never did sums. Trust Miss Boot to spoil things, just when they were getting interesting.

CHAPTER 2

Know-All Nick rubbed his head and glared at Bertie. He would get that smelly scruffbag. Maybe he should put a worm down his back? But that was no good. Bertie wasn't scared of worms, in fact the slimier the better. Maybe he could push him in a muddy puddle? But that wouldn't work either – Bertie *liked* getting muddy.

No, he needed a cunning plan, something that Bertie would never suspect.

Wait, what had Bertie been babbling about earlier? Pirate treasure. Nick smiled to himself slyly. If it was treasure Bertie wanted, he would lead him right to it. All he needed was a map. He checked Miss Boot wasn't looking and tore a sheet from his notepad. Now, where to make Bertie think the loot was buried? Somewhere forbidden like the girls' toilets, or better still… Nick's eyes lit up. He knew the perfect place. Just wait – Bertie was going to be in *so* much trouble!

At lunch break, Bertie and his pirate crew prowled the playground.

"Hello, Bertie!" trilled a voice.

Bertie swung round. Curses, it was Angela Nicely! Angela lived next door and had been in love with him for ever.

"Are you playing pirates?" she asked. "Can I play?"

"No," said Bertie. "Play with your own friends."

"They're playing mummies and daddies," grumbled Angela. "I want to be a pirate!"

"Well you can't," said Bertie. "You're not dressed like a pirate. Anyway, you're a girl."

"Girls can be pirates," said Angela.

"No they can't," said Bertie. "I'm the captain and there are no girls on my ship."

Angela sniffed. "You can't stop me," she said. "If I want to be a pirate then I can, so there!"

Bertie sighed. When he had his own ship Angela would be the first to walk the plank.

Suddenly something whizzed through the air and bounced off his nose.

BOINK!

Bertie looked round. Who dared throw an apple core at the pirate king?

"HA HA!" jeered a weedy voice. "Can't catch me! Na na nee na na!"

Know-All Nick ducked out of sight.

"After him!" yelled Bertie.

The chase was on. It didn't last long because Nick was slower than a grandfather tortoise. Soon he found himself trapped with no escape.

"Stay back! I'll tell Miss Boot!" he panted.

Bertie shook his head. "Not this time, she's not on duty. Feeling ticklish, Nick?"

"You wouldn't!" said Nick.

Bertie grabbed his arm. As Nick squirmed away something fell from his pocket. Darren pounced on it first.

"AHARRR! What's this?" he cried.

"That's mine," said Nick. "Give it back!"

Bertie held out his hand. "Let me see."

He unfolded the piece of paper. It was torn at the edges and brown with dirt.

Bertie stared at it in amazement.

"It's a treasure map!"

They all crowded round.

"Look – a skull and crossbones!" said Bertie excitedly. "That means it's a pirate treasure map."

He turned to Nick. "Where did you get this?"

Nick shrugged. "If you must know, I found it inside an old book."

"I knew it!' said Bertie excitedly. "This is probably thousands of years old."

Darren stared. "You mean there's actual treasure? Like gold and diamonds and stuff?"

"Of course," said Bertie. "And I'll tell you what else, it's buried near by. That's our school field." He pointed to the map.

Bertie and his pirate crew hurried off with Angela tagging behind. Know-All Nick watched them go and smiled to himself. His brilliant plan was working perfectly.

CHAPTER 3

"Right," said Bertie, spreading out the map. "The treasure must be buried somewhere round here." They were standing on the playing field, which Mr Grouch prepared in the summer for cricket.

"But where?" asked Eugene. "We can't dig up the whole field."

"I know!" cried Angela. "It's X marks the spot!"

"I was just about to say that," said Bertie. "It's X marks the spot – that's where pirates always bury their treasure."

"You mean like there?" asked Eugene.

Bertie looked closer at a small black X on the map. Someone had helpfully written "TREJUR" beside it.

"That's it!" Bertie cried. "Let's start digging!"

"Yes, but where exactly?" asked Darren. Bertie frowned. Map reading wasn't really his strong point. He was much better at giving orders.

"What about this clue?" cried Angela, pointing to some words scribbled on the map.

Bertie read it out. "'From Boot's Lookout, twenty paces F.'"

"Makes no sense," said Darren. "What's Boot's Lookout?"

They all looked blank.

"Miss Boot!" cried Eugene. "She always sits in the same place on playground duty."

"The bench!" cried Bertie.

They all hurried over. It was strange that an old pirate treasure map should mention Miss Boot, but Bertie was too busy reading the next part of the clue to worry about that.

"'Twenty paces F.'" He frowned.

"Maybe it's short for something," said Darren. "Like twenty paces Friday."

"Or twenty paces, frog-face!" cried Angela.

"Forwards!" yelled Eugene. "It means twenty paces forward."

Bertie stood with his back to the bench and paced out the steps.

"Seventeen, eighteen, nineteen, tw—" He stopped. They'd reached a small square of grass which was green and freshly mown. It was guarded by a large sign.

"This is it," said Bertie. "We dig here."

"The cricket pitch?" said Darren. "You're joking! Mr Grouch will murder us."

Mr Grouch was very proud of his cricket pitch, which he mowed and watered every week. Anyone caught walking on the grass risked dying a horrible death.

"Well, that's it then," sighed Darren.

"We're not giving up now!" said Bertie. "It's buried treasure!"

"Yes, but what if we get caught?" said Eugene.

"We won't," replied Bertie. "We'll fill in the hole so Mr Grouch will never know."

"Aren't you forgetting one thing?" said Darren. "We haven't got a spade."

Angela jumped up and down excitedly. "I know, I know! Follow me!"

They followed her back to the playground and the caretaker's shed. The door was open, but there was one problem – Mr Grouch. He was round the other side, dozing in his deckchair. Angela tiptoed fearlessly inside. A moment later, she handed three spades through the window.

"What about Grouch?" asked Eugene, as they hurried away. "What if he wakes up and notices his tools are gone."

"Stop worrying," said Bertie. "Someone can keep lookout from the bench."

They took a vote and elected Angela, who only agreed if she was allowed to hold the treasure map.

"If you see Grouch coming, then whistle," Bertie told her.

"Okay, I'll try," said Angela. "But I'm not very good at whistling."

CHAPTER 4

They began to dig. It was harder work than Bertie had expected. After ten minutes they were hot and sweaty.

"I'm tired," grumbled Eugene.

"My arms ache!" moaned Darren.

"Keep going," panted Bertie. "It's got to be here somewhere."

The digging went on. The hole got

deeper and deeper. The pile of earth grew bigger and bigger.

CLUNK!

Bertie stopped. His spade had struck something hard.

"I've found it!" he yelled. "Quick! Help me pull it out!"

They scrabbled in the mud. There was something smooth and heavy, exactly like a treasure chest. *This is it*, thought Bertie, tugging at it. He'd be rich beyond his wildest dreams. Gold, diamonds, rubies... He could buy anything he wanted – a robot, a swimming pool, a year's supply of ice cream...

OOF! They heaved the heavy lump clear. Bertie stared. In front of him was a dirty great rock. He flopped down on the ground, exhausted.

"What's the matter, Bertie?" jeered a reedy voice. "Didn't you find any treasure?"

Know-All Nick stood over him, wearing a sickly smile of triumph.

"I don't understand," moaned Bertie. "The map said to dig right here."

"I know!" sniggered Nick.

"This has to be the place. X marks the spot," said Bertie.

"Oh, it's the right place, all right," grinned Nick. "I should know."

Bertie stared. Slowly, the terrible truth dawned on him. He'd been tricked! There was no treasure. The map was nothing but a rotten fake! That sneaky creep Nick had dreamed up the whole thing.

Just then, Angela Nicely came running up, out of breath.

"Pfft! Pfft!" she blew, trying to whistle.

"Go away!" snapped Nick. "We're busy."

"But listen," panted Angela. "It's..."

"It was you!" shouted Bertie, glaring at Nick.

"Of course it was me," smirked Nick. "I drew the map and made sure you found it. You're so stupid, I knew you'd fall for it."

"But... Why?" said Bertie.

"So you'd get the blame, of course," said Nick. "Wait until Mr Grouch sees his precious cricket pitch. You are so dead!"

"But it's all your fault!" argued Bertie.

"I know," gloated Nick. "But face it, no one's ever going to believe you!"

"Oh really?" growled a deep voice.

Know-All Nick spun round. He turned as white as a sheet. Mr Grouch was standing right behind him, purple with fury.

"I tried to tell you," whispered Angela.

Mr Grouch looked at the hole, then at Nick.

"So this was your clever idea, was it? Well, let's see what Miss Boot has to say about that!"

"B-b-but ... it wasn't me! Bertie dug the hole!" stammered Nick.

Mr Grouch scowled at Bertie and his friends. "As for you lot, I want this hole filled in before I get back."

He frogmarched Nick away, still wailing that he was innocent.

Bertie waited until they'd gone and let out a long breath.

"Um, poor Nick," said Angela.

"Yes, poor old Nick," Bertie nodded. He looked at his pirate crew and broke into a grin.

"AHARRRRR!" they cried.

BURGER!

CHAPTER 1

Bertie was squashed on the sofa with Suzy and Dad, staring at the TV. Captain Thunder was being chased by the Incredible Blob.

"Zap him! Use your lightning laser!" yelled Bertie.

Suddenly Mum burst into the room.

"I've got some exciting news!" she cried.

Bertie looked up. Perhaps school was closed for the week – or, even better, it had burned down? Maybe Miss Boot had been arrested for cruelty to children?

"I've been asked to write for the *Pudsley Post*," said Mum. "They want me to do a weekly restaurant review."

"Fantastic!" said Dad.

"They want you to what?" said Bertie.

"It means I go to a restaurant and write about it in the paper," explained Mum. "They want the first one soon, so I'm booking dinner for Saturday night."

"Great!" said Dad. "Can you take a guest?"

"Yes," said Mum. "And the best part is the paper pays the bill. We get a free meal!"

Bertie pricked up his ears. A FREE meal? Why didn't anyone say so before! He was always willing to eat out for free. What's more he knew the perfect restaurant – Burger Madness. Darren said the Mighty Mega Cheeseburgers were so big he could hardly fit one in his mouth.

"Can you choose any restaurant?" asked Bertie.

"Of course," said Mum.

"Brilliant!" said Bertie.

"Oh no," said Dad. "We're not taking *you*."

Bertie's face fell. "Why not?"

"Because whenever we take you out for dinner it always ends in disaster," said Dad. "Remember last time?"

Bertie did. He'd spilled Coke down Suzy's dress and got a pea stuck up his nose. But that wasn't his fault, it could have happened to anyone!

"This time will be different!" he promised.

"Out of the question," said Dad.

"What about me?" moaned Suzy. "I never get to eat in nice restaurants."

Mum looked at Dad. She'd been hoping for a romantic dinner for two. But it was true, they hardly ever ate out as a family. And if Suzy came they could hardly leave Bertie at home.

"All right," she sighed. "We'll all go."

"YAAAAAY!" whooped Bertie.

"But only on one condition," said Mum. "You're on your best behaviour."

"Okay!" said Bertie.

"And you're not going anywhere until you tidy your room."

"Okay, okay," said Bertie. If it meant he could eat at Burger Madness he was willing to do anything – even tidy his room. He turned back to the TV.

"Well, what are you waiting for?" asked Mum.

"What, *now*?" said Bertie.

"Yes, now," said Mum. "And I'll be up in a minute to check."

CHAPTER 2

Upstairs, Bertie closed his bedroom door and got down on his hands and knees.

"Eric?" he said. "Eric, it's me!"

He reached under the bed and pulled out a goldfish bowl. Inside were a few rocks, some muddy weed and a small green frog. Bertie lifted him out and set him on the carpet. Eric was

Bertie's latest pet. He'd had other pets – but none of them had lasted very long. As soon as Mum found out, she insisted he get rid of them. Eric had come from the pond in the park. Bertie was hoping that one day he'd produce tadpoles, though he wasn't too sure if boy frogs could have babies. In the meantime, he was hoping to train Eric.

Bertie fished out a half-eaten biscuit from his pocket.

"Are you hungry, Eric?"

Eric didn't seem to be. Maybe he didn't like Jammie Dodgers.

Just then, Bertie heard footsteps on the stairs. Uh oh – Mum was coming! If she found Eric there would be big trouble. Bertie shoved the goldfish bowl under the bed and threw a pair of pants over Eric.

"KURAAAAK!"

"Shhh! Be quiet!" hissed Bertie.

A second later, Mum poked her head around the door.

"Bertie, who were you talking to?"

"Me? No one," said Bertie, innocently.

Mum gave him a suspicious look. "You're meant to be tidying your room."

"I am," said Bertie. "I've made a start. I, um … folded my pyjamas."

Mum glanced at his pyjamas which were screwed up on the floor. As usual Bertie's bedroom looked as if it had been hit by a tornado.

Mum pointed. "Are those pants dirty? Why aren't they in the washing basket?"

Bertie looked down. The pair of pants suddenly twitched into life.

"ARGH!" screamed Mum. "There's something there!"

"Where?" said Bertie.

"There! They just moved!"

The pants were getting away – they hopped across the floor in little jumps. Mum had seen enough. She marched over and scooped them up.

"KUURAAAAAK!"

"A FROG!" screeched Mum.

"Oh yes!" said Bertie. "I wonder where he came from."

Mum let out a long sigh. "I've told you a hundred times, Bertie, you are not to keep pets in your room. He'll have to go!"

"But I haven't trained him yet," said Bertie. "And he's hungry."

"All the more reason for him to go outside where he belongs," said Mum.

"Can't I just keep him a few more days?" begged Bertie.

"No!" said Mum. "Take him out to the garden right now."

Bertie trailed out of the back door with Eric cupped in his hands. It was starting to drizzle. He trudged to the bottom of the garden and set the frog down on a big grey stone.

"Sorry, Eric," he sighed. "Mum says you can't stay."

The frog blinked up at him with large, sad eyes.

"I know, but I'm not allowed," said Bertie. "You'll be okay, won't you?"

"KUURAAAAK!"

Bertie stroked his head one last time, then turned and plodded back to the house. When he looked round, Eric hadn't moved. Bertie sighed. It was cruel to leave him in a strange garden, especially with next door's cat sniffing around. He'd be much happier back at the pond. Bertie glanced at the house … no one was watching. Maybe he'd keep Eric for another day or two – just till he could return him to the park.

CHAPTER 3

On Saturday night, everyone got ready to go to the restaurant. Bertie had managed to keep Eric hidden all week, but he was worried about his pet frog. Eric hadn't touched the Choc-o-Pops he'd saved him from breakfast. Bertie had decided there was only one thing to do.

At seven o'clock Bertie's family bundled into the car and set off.

"Remember, Bertie – behave or you're going straight home," warned Mum.

"You said!" groaned Bertie.

"Use your knife and fork," said Mum.

"And don't play with your food," said Dad.

"And if you spill anything down my dress I'll scream," added Suzy.

Bertie rolled his eyes. If he'd known his family were going to make this much fuss he'd have stayed at home. Anyone would think they were having tea with the Queen! Up ahead he could see the flashing sign of Burger Madness. He already knew what he was going to order: a Mighty Mega Cheeseburger with extra fries and no salad. He could almost taste it now, a big juicy burger swimming in... Wait a minute, they'd driven straight past! Where was Mum going? The car turned right and came to a stop.

"Here we are!" cried Mum. "Restaurant Paradiso!"

Bertie stared. "But I thought we were going to Burger Madness!"

Mum laughed. "Whatever gave you that idea?"

"You said we could go anywhere we liked," moaned Bertie.

"That's right," said Mum. "And I chose Restaurant Paradiso. It's new and very smart."

Bertie climbed out of the car and drooped to the door. He didn't want to eat at Restaurant Paradiso. He bet they only served the kind of sloppy gunk his parents liked to eat.

He trailed inside and looked around. A piano tinkled in the background. People sat at tables peering at their food by candlelight.

"Oooh, isn't it nice?" cooed Mum.

Bertie snorted. If he'd wanted to sit in the dark he could have gone to the cinema.

The head waiter stepped forward to greet them.

"Good evening sir, madam. May I take your coats?"

"Um … no thanks," said Bertie quickly.

He was wearing his blue jumper that he'd chosen for a special reason. It had a large front pocket – big enough to hide a frog. After all, he could hardly leave Eric at home to starve!

The waiter showed them to their table and brought the menu. Bertie read it gloomily.

Chicken on a Bed of Gloop
Vegetables in Sickly Slop
Smelly Fish Cooked in Gloopy Gunk.

"Mmm, it all sounds delicious!" said Mum.

"I can't decide what to have!" said Suzy.

"I know what I want," said Bertie. "Cheeseburger and chips."

"They don't have cheeseburgers," sighed Dad. "Or chips. This is a smart restaurant. Take your elbows off the table and sit up."

Bertie scowled. At Burger Madness everything came with chips. Burger with chips, cheeseburger with chips, chips with chips. If he leaned forward he could see the restaurant's brightly-lit windows across the road. Suddenly something tickled his leg.

"AH HOO HA HAA!" he giggled.

"Shh!" hissed Mum. "What's the matter with you?"

"Nothing," said Bertie. "I've just got a … HEE HA HA!"

"BERTIE! STOP IT!" snapped Dad.

Bertie lifted the tablecloth to look. Help! Eric had escaped from his pocket and was exploring his leg. Bertie reached out to grab him, but the frog sprang off, landing on the floor. Uh-oh. Now what? How was he going to rescue Eric without his parents noticing?

Mum leaned forward and lowered her voice. "Don't look now," she said, "but I'm sure that's Gerald Fusspot at the next table."

"Who?" said Suzy.

"You know, the famous food critic. He's on TV."

Bertie looked over. At the next table was a plump man with the hairiest moustache he'd ever seen. The waiters hovered round him like flies.

"Bertie, don't stare. It's rude!" hissed Mum.

Bertie sighed. This was the last time he came to a posh restaurant. You couldn't move without someone telling you off! But right now he had other things to worry about. He needed to capture Eric.

Just then, the waiter arrived. Bertie ordered the first thing on the menu – Chicken on a Bed of Gloop. While his parents were busy talking, he ducked under the tablecloth. He stared in horror. No! Where was Eric? He could be anywhere. If Mum saw him she would go bananas.

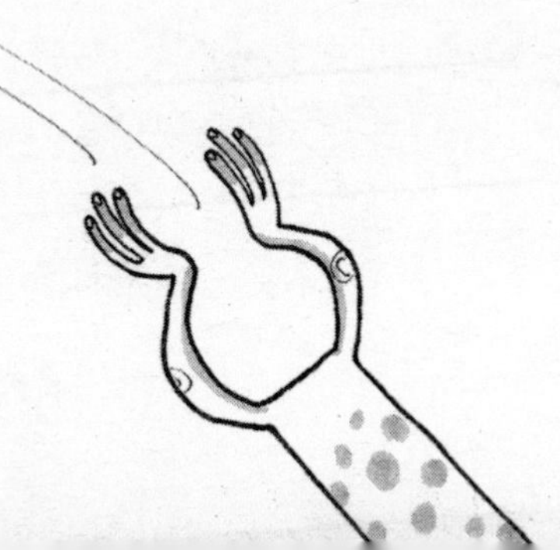

CHAPTER 4

Bertie scanned the restaurant. Eric couldn't have gone far. He was probably just hiding under a chair or … ARGH! There he was – on Gerald Fusspot's table! Fusspot was reading a book while he waited for his dessert. He hadn't noticed Eric yet. Bertie jumped to his feet.

"Do you ever keep still?" groaned Mum.

"Yes … no … I um … need the toilet," Bertie mumbled.

"Now?" said Mum. "Your food will be here any minute."

"I won't be long," said Bertie.

He made his way towards the toilets. As he passed Fusspot's table, Bertie bent down pretending to tie his shoelace. Good, no one was paying him any attention. Dropping to all fours, he crawled over to the table and peeped above it. Eric blinked back at him. Slowly, Bertie's hand slid across the table, ready to grab him.

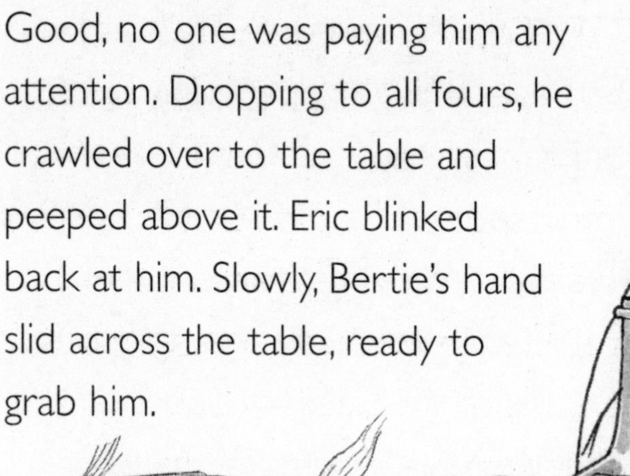

Just at that moment, a waiter arrived with a large bowl. "Your dessert, sir."

Bertie ducked out of sight. Where was Eric now? As the waiter disappeared he risked another peek. Gerald Fusspot was helping himself to a large spoonful of raspberry trifle. As he raised it to his mouth, two small beady eyes met his own.

"YARRGH!" he yelled. "A FROG!"

Then everything happened at once. An old lady screamed. Mum looked over and spotted Bertie. All the waiters came running. One of them tried to flatten Eric with an enormous ladle.

THUMP! WHAM! BANG!

Bertie shot out of his hiding place.

"STOP!" he cried. "I'll catch him!"

But Eric had other ideas. He hopped around the table like a jumping bean. CRASH! Bowls, plates and a bottle of wine hit the floor. Eric made a flying leap and landed on Fusspot's head.

"AAARGHH!"

"Don't move!" cried Bertie. He picked up the pudding bowl and crept closer, ready to pounce.

"GOT YOU!" he cried, slamming it down.

There was an awkward silence. Mum gasped. Dad groaned. A trickle of cream was running down the famous critic's head and dripping from his nose. Bertie lifted the bowl to peep underneath.

"Whoops!" he said. "Anyone seen a frog?"

Half an hour later, Bertie's family still weren't talking to him. The manager had ordered them to leave and never come back. Bertie couldn't see why everyone was so upset. It was only a frog, after all. The way Gerald Fusspot went on you'd have thought he'd been savaged by a tiger!

Still, it wasn't all bad. He'd managed to rescue Eric. And Mum still had her review to write, so they'd had to find another restaurant. Luckily, it turned out there was one place that still had room.

"Yes," said the waitress. "What can I get you?"

"A Mighty Mega Cheeseburger, please," said Bertie. "With extra fries."

RUN!

CHAPTER 1

"FASTER!" bellowed Miss Boot. "I SAID RUN, BERTIE, NOT WALK!"

Bertie groaned and broke into a trot. Teachers were always telling you off for running in the corridor. But when it was PE they shouted at you for NOT running. Why didn't they make up their minds? He trailed across the playing field and flopped down on the grass, coming in last.

"Some of you need to try harder," said Miss Boot, eyeing Bertie. "Now, while you're all getting your breath back, I have some exciting news. Next Friday is our School Sports Day."

"Hooray! Sports Day!" cheered the class.

Brilliant! thought Bertie. Sports Day meant a whole day off boring lessons. Best of all it meant medals. Darren had won two last year and he'd worn them every day for a week. Bertie had never won a medal. The closest he'd come was fourth in the egg and spoon race. This year would be different, though. He was determined to get his hands on a shiny winners' medal. It was just a matter of finding a race he could win.

"So pay attention," said Miss Boot. "I'm going to read through the list of races. Put up your hand if you would like to take part."

Everyone sat up eagerly. If you didn't get one of the good races, you might end up in the beanbag challenge or the blindfold race (last year Eugene had walked into a tree).

"The 60 metre sprint," said Miss Boot. "Who'd like to take part in this one?"

"Ooh, miss, miss!" cried the whole class, waving their hands in the air.

Bertie kept quiet. There was no way he would ever win a sprint against Zoe Trotter. She was faster than a bionic greyhound.

"The three-legged race?" said Miss Boot.

Bertie frowned. With his luck he'd probably get paired with weedy Trevor or worse, Know-All Nick. Better to choose a race he could win on his own.

Miss Boot droned on. The chariot race, the obstacle race, the backwards hopping race… By the time she'd finished, everyone was in a race – or almost everyone.

Bertie's hand went up.

"What about me, miss?"

Miss Boot groaned. "Didn't you put up your hand like everyone else?"

"No," said Bertie.

"Well, why not?"

"Because there wasn't a race I liked," said Bertie.

Miss Boot ground her teeth. Why was it always Bertie? She looked down her list – most of the races were full.

"Will your parents be coming?" she asked.

"I s'pect so," said Bertie.

"Good, then I'll put you down for the parent-child relay," said Miss Boot.

"What?" cried Bertie.

"Don't say 'what'!" snapped Miss Boot. "It's a relay race, Bertie. You'll be in a team with one of your parents."

Bertie gaped. Was Miss Boot mad? His *parents*? He'd stand more chance of winning with a stuffed gorilla.

"But … but they're OLD!" he protested.

"I'm sure they'll be fine," said Miss Boot. "Just make sure one of them will be there."

Bertie slumped back on the grass. This was terrible. Parents came to Sports Day to watch, not to take part! It would be so embarrassing! And besides, how was he going to win a medal if he was stuck with his mum or dad?

CHAPTER 2

At supper that evening, Bertie brought up the subject with his parents.

"It's our school Sports Day next Friday," he began. "You are coming, aren't you?"

"Of course," said Mum. "We always come."

"Only Miss Boot's picked me for the relay," said Bertie.

"Don't talk with your mouth full," said Mum. "What relay?"

"The parent-child relay," said Bertie.

"That'll be fun," grinned Dad. "Who's the parent?"

"Well, you are," said Bertie. "I said you'd take part."

A lump of mash dropped off Dad's fork.

"You want me to run a relay race – with *you*?" he said.

"Yes," said Bertie.

Mum and Suzy burst out laughing.

"I don't see what's so funny," said Bertie, scowling.

"I'm sorry," said Mum, wiping her eyes. "It's just the idea of your dad running a race."

"What's funny about that?" said Dad.

"I used to play football you know."

"When? At junior school?" giggled Suzy.

"Anyway," said Mum. "I notice you didn't ask me, Bertie."

"No way," said Bertie. "I want to win!"

"Thanks a lot," sniffed Mum. "Maybe you and I should enter, Suzy?"

Bertie snorted. Now that would be funny – his mum and Suzy in a relay race! The last time he'd seen Mum run was when she found a spider in the bath.

He turned back to Dad. "But anyway, can you come?"

Dad grunted. "Hmm. I'm not sure."

"But you've got to! I've told Miss Boot!" cried Bertie. "And it's my only chance to win a medal!"

"We'll see," said Dad. "Work's very busy right now."

Dirty Bertie

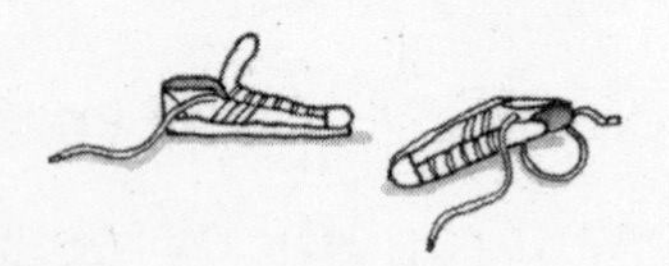

After supper Dad went out to cut the front hedge. Mum reminded Bertie that Whiffer hadn't been out for a walk. Bertie was just closing the front gate when he was almost flattened by someone running past.

"Oh, hello, Bertie!"

Bertie groaned. It was Royston Rich. Royston was the biggest show-off in the class and

Bertie couldn't stand him. He was wearing a bright red tracksuit exactly like his dad's. They both jogged on the spot.

"Me and Dad are on a training run," panted Royston.

"Really?" said Bertie.

"Yes," said Mr Rich. "I try to run every day. You know, just four or five miles."

"Is that all?" said Dad, coming to join them.

"Do you run yourself?" asked Mr Rich.

"Not really," said Dad. "I don't have time."

"Pity, you should keep in shape," said Mr Rich. "At your age."

Bertie stared. Mr Rich was smiling smugly while Dad glared back at him. They looked as if they might start a fight.

Whiffer pulled at his lead, sniffing round Mr Rich's legs. Bertie hoped he didn't mistake him for a lamp post.

"Well, must get on," said Mr Rich. "We've got an important race next week."

"Oh? What's that?" said Bertie.

"The parent-child relay race," said Royston. "Me and my dad are a team."

"That's funny, so are we!" said Dad.

"Are we?" said Bertie.

"Splendid!" said Mr Rich, stroking his moustache. "I like a bit of competition. But I warn you now, I don't like losing."

"Nor do I," said Dad.

The Riches turned to go.

"See you, smelly-pants," said Royston.

"See you, goofy," said Bertie.

He watched them jog off down the road, then turned to Dad.

"I thought you said you couldn't come?"

"I changed my mind," said Dad. "I'm not going to be beaten by that stuck-up twerp."

"No," said Bertie. "But they look like they're taking it pretty seriously."

"Fine," said Dad. "Two can play at that game. First thing tomorrow morning you and me start training."

CHAPTER 3

At 7a.m. the next morning Dad dragged Bertie out of bed. Bertie groaned. He didn't want to go for a training run. He had important stuff to do on Saturdays, like watching TV.

They jogged out of the gate and along the road. After one lap of the park Dad needed to sit down. He slumped on a bench with his head between his knees, gasping for breath.

"You've gone all red in the face," said Bertie.

"I'll be okay," panted Dad. "Just … need … a minute."

"Can we get an ice cream?" asked Bertie.

Dad shook his head; he seemed to have lost his voice. Just then, two joggers came running along the path. Bertie groaned. It was the Riches again. They seemed to be following them.

"You okay, old chap?" said Mr Rich, slowing down. "You look a bit hot."

"I'm fine," wheezed Dad. "Just doing a few stretches."

"Nice shorts, Bertie," grinned Royston. "How many laps have you done?"

"Five or six," lied Bertie.

"We're doing twenty," bragged Royston. "My dad's super fit. He's running the marathon this year."

"Big deal," said Bertie.

"Your dad doesn't even go jogging," sneered Royston.

"So what? He could beat your dad any day!" said Bertie.

"Fat chance," scoffed Royston.

"Come on, Royston," said Mr Rich.

"Let these chaps get their breath back. See you on Sports Day then. Should be fun!"

"Bye bye, Bertie!" jeered Royston. "If you're lucky, I'll show you my winners' medal!"

Dad scowled after them as they sped off. "I can't stand that man," he said.

"You're lucky you're not in Royston's class," sighed Bertie. "If they win this race I'll never hear the last of it."

"They're not going to win," said Dad, getting to his feet. "Come on, just three more laps."

Half an hour later they arrived home. Bertie practically had to carry his dad into the house.

"What happened to you?" asked Mum.

"We went jogging," explained Bertie. "Dad's a bit puffed out."

"My legs!" moaned Dad. "My back!" He hobbled to the sofa and collapsed with a groan. Mum shook her head.

"Aren't you taking this all a bit seriously?" she asked. "It's only a school Sports Day!"

"Yes, but Royston Rich and his dad have entered," explained Bertie. "We have to beat them."

"Ah," said Mum. "I might have known. Well, you boys had better watch out because Suzy and I have put our names down."

"For what?" said Bertie.

"The relay race," said Mum. "So Royston and his dad aren't your only competition."

"Ha ha, very funny," said Bertie. This was getting ridiculous – his whole family were taking part! Still, he couldn't wait to see Suzy and Mum come in last.

CHAPTER 4

Sports Day finally arrived. The sun shone. The field was hung with bunting. Miss Boot checked her programme. So far the day was going smoothly. No one had been sick or fainted in the heat. A dozen races had come and gone without a hitch. Now it was time for the final race of the day – the parent-child relay. Miss Boot's face clouded over. She'd just remembered who was taking part. But surely not even Bertie could ruin a simple relay race? She blew on her whistle and called everyone to the starting line.

Bertie stood with his dad eyeing the other teams. Royston and Mr Rich were busy warming up. They wore matching running vests with a number one on the front. Mum was chatting idly to Suzy. She hadn't even bothered to get changed.

"Last chance to back out," smirked Royston.

"Forget it," said Bertie. "We're going to batter you."

"Oh, I don't think so," said Royston.

Miss Boot explained the rules. There were two parts to the relay. The first leg was a 100 metre sprint for the mums and dads. Then they partnered their children for a wheelbarrow race to the finish.

Bertie, Royston and the others took up their positions further down the track. The parents lined up on the start. Mr Rich crouched forward. Dad hitched up his shorts. Mum gave Suzy a cheery wave. Miss Boot raised her megaphone to her lips.

"On your marks, get set, GO!"

Mr Rich streaked away as if his shorts were on fire.

"COME ON, GERALD!" screeched Mrs Rich, jumping up and down in wild excitement by the finish line.

"Go, Dad! RUN!" yelled Bertie.

He groaned. Already his dad was trailing Mr Rich. Bertie would have to make up ground in the wheelbarrow race. He got down on his hands and knees, ready to go.

Mr Rich reached them first and grabbed his son's legs.

"Ow, you're hurting me!" moaned Royston.

Seconds later Bertie's dad arrived, red-faced and gasping.

"Hurry! Catch them!" cried Bertie.

"I'm trying!" panted Dad.

They set off in pursuit with Bertie walking on his hands. He was good at the wheelbarrow race. He'd practised in the garden with Darren. Just ahead, Royston's team were tiring. Bertie could hear Mr Rich muttering under his breath.

"Move, Royston, they're catching up!"

"It's not my fault!" whined Royston.

"Come *on*, Gerald! Come *on*, Royston!" screamed Mrs Rich.

But Bertie's team were gaining. He could see the finish line up ahead with Miss Darling and Mr Weakly holding the winning tape. Now they were neck and neck. Bertie could hear Royston panting like a dog. Suddenly, his rival swerved across his lane, barging into him.

"ARGH!" Bertie fell flat on his face.

"Bye bye, loser!" crowed Royston, as he pulled away. But he spoke too soon. Bertie's dad wasn't letting them get away with that. He dived for Mr Rich, rugby tackling him from behind.

"OOOOF!"

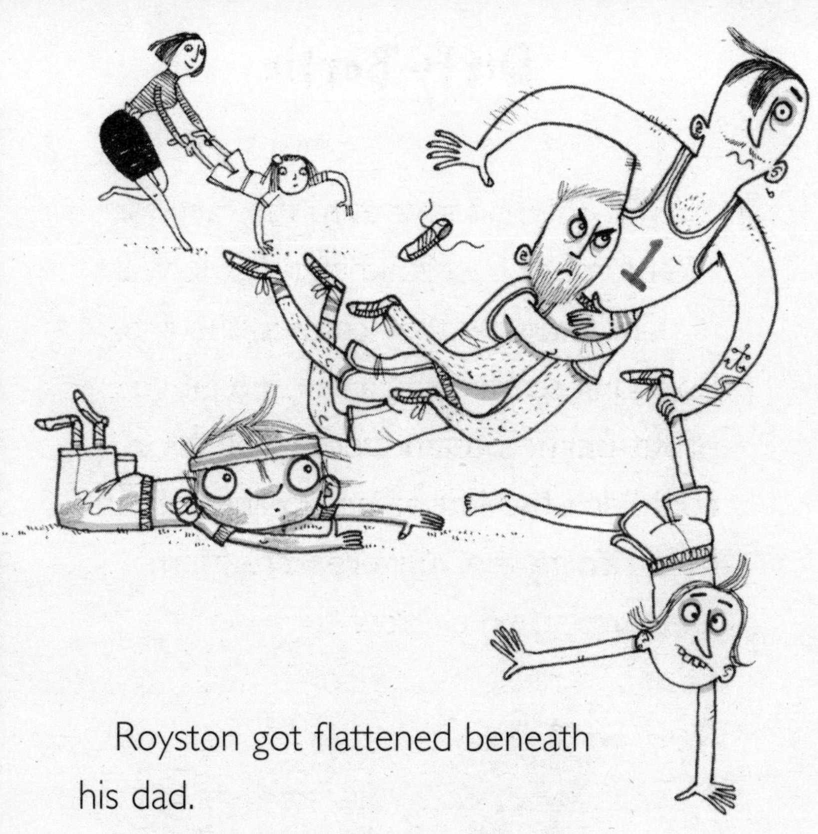

Royston got flattened beneath his dad.

"OWW! Get off!" he wailed.

Miss Boot covered her eyes. The crowd gawped. Bertie and Royston were rolling on the ground, while their dads yelled and shoved each other.

"Cheat!"

"You're the cheat, fat face!"

"Don't you call me fat face!"

Everyone had forgotten the race for the moment. Everyone except the team in third place. As they crossed the line, loud cheers filled the air. Bertie let go of Royston's foot and looked up. No, it couldn't be! After all that effort, all that training, the winners were Mum and Suzy!